THIS BLOOMSBURY BOOK

BELONGS TO

....

To Freya, without whom this book would never have happened.

With love, Mummy

BLOOMSBURY
CHILDREN'S
BOOKS

First published in Great Britain in 2002 by Bloomsbury Publishing Plc
38 Soho Square, London, W1D 3HB
This paperback edition first published in 2003

A CIP catalogue record of this book is available from the British Library

ISBN 0 7475 6121 4

Printed in Belgium by Proost nv

3 5 7 9 10 8 6 4 2

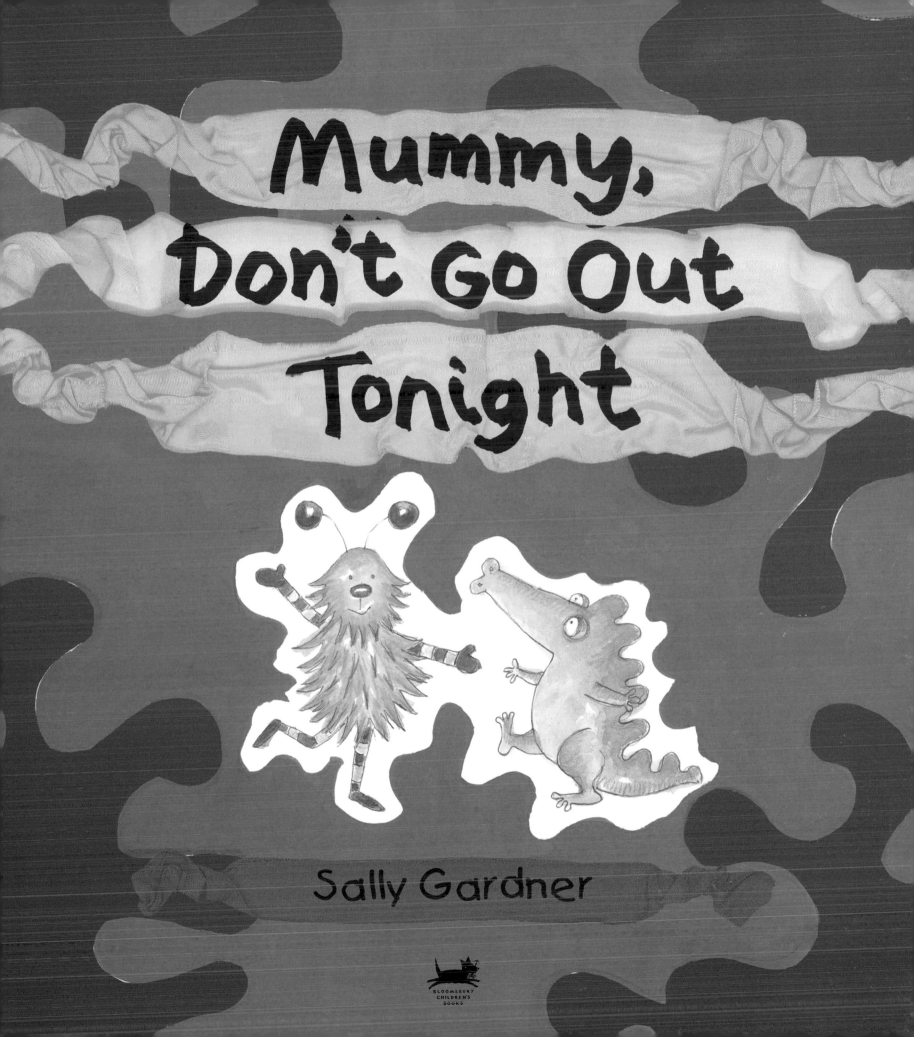

Mummy, Don't Go Out Tonight

Sally Gardner

BLOOMSBURY
CHILDREN'S
BOOKS

"Mummy, Mummy,
don't go out tonight."

'You will be all right.
Daisy will be here."

"Why can't I come with you?"

"Because it's night time
and night time is grown-up time."

"But I need you all the time."

"I know, poppet, I know."

"Monster's going to miss you.
Cat's going to miss you."

"The house will feel so funny without you. I am going to miss you so so so."

"Give me a kiss now. I have to go."

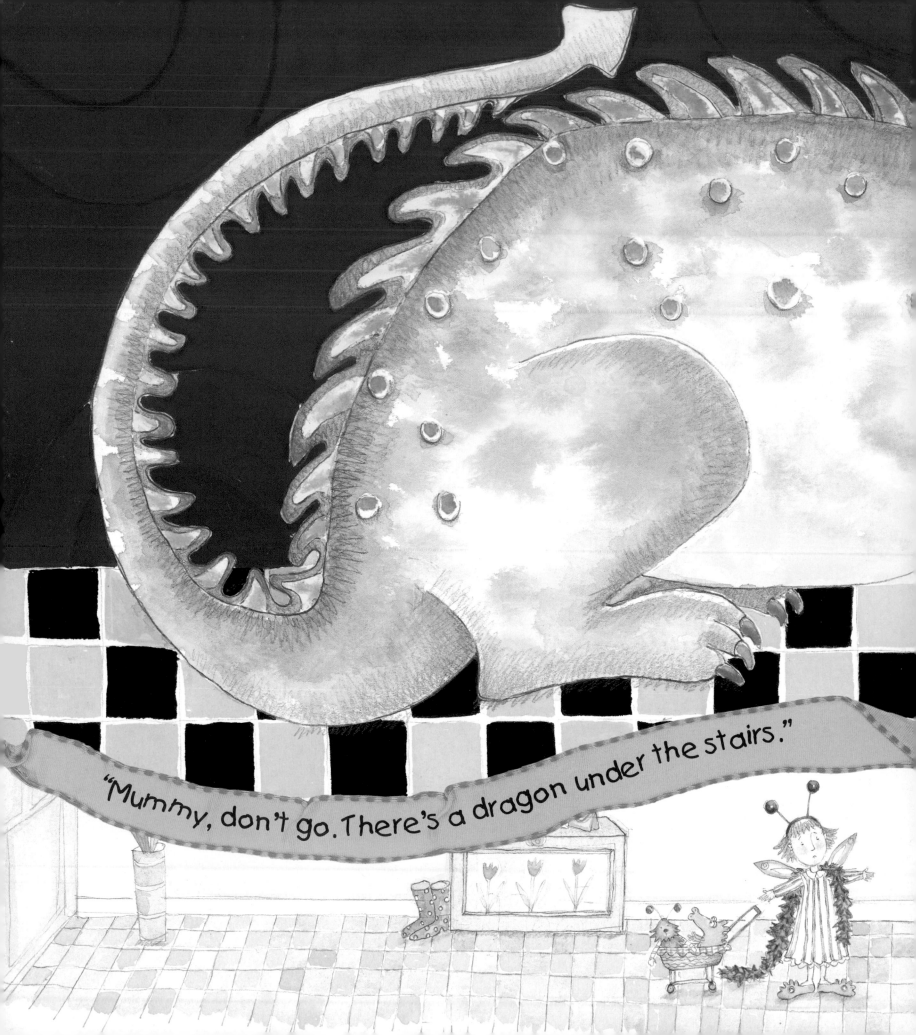

"Mummy, don't go. There's a dragon under the stairs."

"No, poppet, only the hoover lives there."

"Mummy, you might be kidnapped by pirates."

"No, darling, there are no pirates where I'm going."

"You won't run away to the circus?"

"Poppet, don't be silly. No circus would have me!"

"Mummy, a giant could take you away and a monster

might eat you up." "I don't think so!"

"The cat could have kittens."   "She's far too old for that."

"Darling, everything is going to be all right.

Give me a kiss! Night-night."

"Daisy, may I have four fishfingers?

One for me and two for Monster and one for my dragon."

"Daisy, shall we go dancing? I will dress up.

I'll be a princess and you can be the prince."

"Daisy, will you read to me? This book and another one?

Is it long now, till Mummy is home?"

"Daisy, will you come again? Monster likes you being here,

I like you being here. Daisy, will you sit with me until I go to sleep?"

"Sweet dreams, my poppet. Sleep tight."

Enjoy more great picture books from Bloomsbury ...

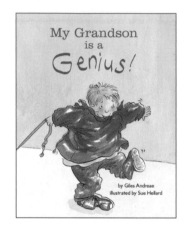

MY GRANDSON IS A GENIUS!
Giles Andreae & Sue Hellard

BAD HARE DAY
Miriam Moss & Lynne Chapman

JACK AND THE DREAMSACK
Laurence Anholt & Ross Collins

POLLY'S PICNIC
Richard Hamilton & Sophy Williams